COMING HOME

To Lynne, for ever

While this book is based on real characters and actual historical events,
some situations and people are fictional, created by the author.

Scholastic Children's Books,
Euston House, 24 Eversholt Street,
London NW1 1DB, UK

A division of Scholastic Ltd
London ~ New York ~ Toronto ~ Sydney ~ Auckland
Mexico City ~ New Delhi ~ Hong Kong

First published in the UK by Scholastic Ltd, 2018

ISBN 978 1407 18668 9

Text © Jim Eldridge, 2018
. Cover artwork © Two Dots

Printed and bound by
CPI Group (UK) Ltd, Croydon, CR0 4YY

2 4 6 8 10 9 7 5 3 1

Papers used by Scholastic Children's Books
are made from wood grown in sustainable forests.

www.scholastic.co.uk

JIM ELDRIDGE

COMING HOME

SCHOLASTIC

CHAPTER

Peeeeep!

Dawn, 4th November 1918, and the shrill blast of the lieutenant's whistle sent us out of the deep, muddy trench where we'd spent the night, up the wooden ladders and over the top. Ahead of us, on the other side of the Sambre–Oise canal, was the German defensive line – but we had to cross open fields to get to it.

Tacka-tacka-tacka-tacka! The German machine guns opened fire as soon as they saw us, as did their rifles, and bullets tore into us. Some of the men either side of me stumbled and fell, but we kept going. We ducked low and weaved from side to side, opening fire ourselves. Our unit's commanding officer, Lieutenant Owen, was right at the front, leading the charge and urging us on. Bullets thudded into the earth at my feet, sailing past me so close that one tore at the sleeve of my uniform.

Bang! Bang! I fired back and kept going. Nearer and nearer we got to the canal. We were making for a place where there was a lock, but the Germans had put a machine gun inside the lockhouse and the rapid fire was tearing into our advance, with more soldiers falling the closer we got.

We'd been *told* that the Germans were in retreat and that they'd only left a handful of soldiers to hold the canal, to allow most of their forces to move further back for a last stand. But we'd been told that before and it had been wrong.

We ran on, firing, getting ever closer.

I saw a flash as a hand grenade was thrown from our side towards the lockhouse. Flames and thick black smoke belched out of the lockhouse window. Another grenade followed. German soldiers stumbled out of the lockhouse and ran to dive behind cover. But they were soon firing at us again.

Some of our Royal Engineers had reached the lock and were laying ladders across the open lock gate to make a bridge to the other side. More ladders were dropped into place, while our troops gave the Engineers covering fire.

We dropped down to the ground, lying as flat as we could and using whatever we could find for cover – a low mound of earth, a small bush – while we fired at the Germans on the other side of the canal. We had them trapped in their defensive positions while our forces crawled across the ladders to the German side. Some didn't make it, tumbling down into the waters of the canal as rifle fire struck them, but more and more managed to cross and attack the German positions from behind.

More ladders appeared, more crossing points opening up across the canal. We were gaining ground! I saw Lieutenant Owen rise up next to me and wave at us to move forward, breaking into a run. We got to our feet and followed him, firing as we advanced.

But the Germans weren't giving up just yet. They returned fire, machine guns and rifles blasting, tearing into our front line. Lieutenant Owen, who was just a few paces in front of me, staggered and fell, crumpling on to his rifle as bullets cut him down. But we ran on.

Some of the Germans stood up behind their defences to get a shot at our soldiers, who were coming at them from the sides and the rear. When they realized they were surrounded, some of them threw down their rifles and put their hands in the air to surrender. Soon the others did the same.

The Battle of the Sambre–Oise canal was over.

CHAPTER

My name is Joe Henry. I was with the 2nd Battalion of the Manchester Regiment. I joined up in July 1918, telling the recruiting sergeant that I was eighteen. The truth is I'm thirteen, but I've always been big for my age. I thought that as long as I didn't talk much about myself to the other blokes, and give clues that I was a lot younger than I looked, I could get away with it. And so far, I had.

I was sure my best mate in the Manchesters, Bob Taylor, suspected the truth. He used to try and trick me with questions about where in Carlisle I lived, and who I knew. He was from Oldham, just outside Manchester, and said he knew people in Carlisle. Once he even asked me directly: "How old actually are you, Joe?" But when I said, "As old as me feet and a bit older than me teeth," he just grinned and gave it up.

The reason I volunteered was because of my dad, Walter. He joined up in 1914, when the war started. He came home for a bit in 1916 after he got gassed in the trenches, but then he went back again. He said he had to do it for King and country. Me mam, Doris, tried to get him to change his mind. She said he'd done enough for his country and he'd die if he went back, especially because his lungs had been damaged by the gas. But Dad has always been stubborn. He says being stubborn is what makes the people of Cumberland who they are. They don't give up, no matter what gets thrown at them. I suppose that's true, I can be stubborn as well, once I get an idea into my head. Like going to war.

Dad went back to the front late in 1916, and by the start of 1918 the war was still going on with no sign of it ending. And that's when I got the idea: I'd go to the war myself and help it be finished quicker. Then Dad could come back home. Conscription had been introduced in 1916, so I knew I'd be called up to join the army when I was eighteen. But that was five years away. I couldn't wait that long.

I told Mam my idea, but she just said not to say silly things like that. She said it would just put false hope into the heads of my six-year-old brother, Tim, and my little sister, Ann, who's four, about Dad coming home soon.

"And don't let me hear you talking about going off to war again. You could get badly wounded! Or die!" She glared at me furiously, her eyes glittering. "It's bad enough your dad being away, I don't want to lose you too."

"I'd be all right," I assured her. "I can look after myself."

"Stop it this instant, Joe," she said, holding up her hand. "Anyway, they wouldn't take you. You have to be eighteen to join up."

Although I knew that was true, I also knew of at least four boys in Carlisle who'd joined up by lying about their age. Danny Mays, a boy who lived on our street, had managed it and he was only two years older than me.

"I'm sure the recruiting sergeant knew I was under age," Danny told me afterwards. "He winked at me when I told him I was eighteen and said, 'Welcome to the army, son'."

Like I said, I've always been big for my age. I'm tall enough to pass as a man, and when my voice broke I thought I had a good chance of getting away with it. I thought that if I joined our local regiment, the Lonsdales, Mam would just march down to the barracks and drag me home. Instead, I went down to Manchester, where my cousin Eric lives, and used his address to join up with the Manchester Regiment. I didn't want Mam to get suspicious so I told her I was going to stay with Eric for a while because he needed some help with his coal business. I didn't want her to worry; she had enough on her hands with working at the munitions factory at Eastriggs near Gretna, and looking after my little brother and sister. It was only after I'd done my basic training and was about to be sent to France that I sent her a postcard telling her I was off to war. I posted it on the way to the ship and tried not to think about her face when it arrived through our letter box.

Our unit arrived in France in the middle of August. We were told that the Germans were retreating but were stuck on the Hindenberg Line, which was a defensive line of troops and weapons between France and Germany they'd built at the start of the war, and then extended as the war went on. Well, if they were in retreat there didn't seem to be much sign of it. We were sent to fight them.

Nothing I'd read about or imagined had prepared me for what real war is like. The first time I saw the bodies on no-man's land, I was sick. And the second. But we all got hardened to it in the end. We just got on with what we were there to do, which was to fight, and do our best to stay alive.

In early September, things began to change. Our armies broke through the Hindenberg Line and started to force the Germans back. I say 'our armies', because it wasn't just the British army. We were fighting alongside French, Belgian, Australian, Indian and New Zealand soldiers, as well as the Americans, who had joined the war at the start of 1917.

By the end of September and early in October, the Germans were heading backwards, although they were fighting all the way. I often wondered if Dad was anywhere nearby. Did he know that I was out here fighting alongside him? Mam could have written to tell him what I'd done, but the army censor might have cut that bit out. They didn't want soldiers being upset by bad news. Bob said the real reason they censored all our letters was to hide the truth from us. He said if we knew about the stupid decisions our generals made, we'd shoot them ourselves.

Sergeant Blake overheard Bob say that and he got really angry. He said if Bob ever repeated those things, he'd have him up on a charge of treason and shot. I didn't think he really would, because Bob was one of the best and bravest men in our regiment and Sergeant Blake would have been stupid to lose him. All the same, Bob was careful about what he said after that. Some of our own side had been shot for saying similar things. They called it mutiny in the ranks.

I don't know if Bob was right or wrong about the generals and the top army brass, because I never had anything to do with them. Most of the officers

I came across were all right, but then they were junior officers like Lieutenant Owen, who'd died during our attack on the canal. Bob and I thought he was a hero. He had led our unit in October when we stormed a German defensive position on the Hindenberg Line. It was 1st October at the town of Joncourt. It had been near a canal, just like today's assault, and we had overrun it, taking loads of Germans prisoner.

After that battle, Bob told me that Lieutenant Owen was actually a poet back in England.

"Wilfred Owen's his proper name," Bob told me. "My wife says he's getting a name for himself among the literary people."

"I've never heard of him," I said.

"Well, you're not literary, are you?" said Bob.

"I can read and write," I told him indignantly.

"*Literary*, not literate." Bob snorted. "Anyway, my sister says it's the London lot who like him. You people from the sticks in Cumberland only know about sheep, not poetry."

"Yes we do!" I retorted. "We've got a poet."

"Who?"

"William Wordsworth. He writes about daffodils."

"There you are, then. Country stuff. My sister says Lieutenant Owen writes about the war. And the war like it really is, not the way some poets write about being brave and such, to make everyone feel better."

"If he writes about how it really is, he'd better be careful," I said. "Sergeant Blake will report him for mutiny in the ranks and have him shot."

And now Lieutenant Owen was dead, shot anyway. He was a very brave man, and – as an officer – fair to us ordinary soldiers. I decided that when I got home I'd see if they had any of his poems at the library in Carlisle.

CHAPTER

After the victory at Sambre, I thought we'd continue with the advance, pushing the Germans right back and forcing them to surrender. As it turned out, our regiment was going to do that, along with the French, Canadians, Americans, Australians and New Zealanders. But Sergeant Blake called me and Bob and ten others and told us we'd be doing what he called 'special duties'.

"I bet it's something rotten," muttered Bob after Sergeant Blake had gone. "Something dangerous that no one else wants to do."

We were allocated a lorry. Sergeant Blake sat up front with the driver. The rest of us sat on long wooden boxes in the back loaded down with our rifles and ammunition, mess kit and kitbags.

The canvas at the back of the lorry had been rolled up, so although we couldn't see where we were going, we could see where we'd been. We soon worked out that we were heading south-west, back into France and away from the Hindenberg Line.

"I don't like it," said Bob. "Why are we going away from where all the action is?"

"Maybe we're being sent home," said Nipper Read. "Maybe the war's over, only they haven't told us yet."

At his words, my heart gave a happy beat. Maybe he was right! Maybe we were going home! That meant Dad would be going home too, and we'd all be together again.

"No chance," said Bob. "If that was the case they'd tell us. They only ever tell us good news."

That wiped the smile off my face. It was true.

We travelled over bumpy roads for hours, with toilet stops now and then, and a break for a bite of bread and cheese and a mug of tea. Finally we left the main roads and bounced over tracks, until we entered a forest, thick with trees.

"I don't like this," said Bob. "Forests mean trouble."

The lorry slowed down, and then gave an extra jolt as we crossed over a railway line. Everyone was silent now. What were our special duties?

"Maybe we're going to be a firing squad," suggested Terry Watts. "Maybe they've rounded up some top German generals and they're going to be shot, but it has to be done in secret. A forest would be the perfect place for it."

"I didn't sign up to be no executioner," said Bob. "I saw enough of that when we was in the trenches. Shooting those poor kids from our own side who didn't want to fight any more so they refused to go over the top. Cowardice in the face of the enemy, they called it. I saw one kid so scared he couldn't stand. Fourteen, he was. He'd lied about his age so he could join up, and when he found out that war wasn't a game, he didn't want to do it any more." He shook his head. "It was because he was poor. When it happens to the rich ones, the officers, it's called shell shock and they get sent back home to a comfy hospital. It ain't fair."

Suddenly the hatch between the back of the lorry and the driver's compartment slid open and Sergeant Blake shouted through it.

"I can hear you, Private Taylor!" he said. "Any more of that kind of talk and you'll be the one on the sharp end of a firing squad. Mutiny and treason!"

The hatch slammed shut, and Bob scowled and shrugged. We all knew he was right. It was just like he said, and it wasn't fair. Soldiers from poor homes who couldn't carry on fighting were shot by a firing squad to discourage anyone else who was thinking of refusing to fight. But the posh rich ones – and that meant most of the officers – were sent back home to recover.

I thought about the fourteen-year-old boy who had been shot. He was a year older than me and he'd lied about his age, same as I did. He had thought war would be fun and exciting.

Me and my best friend, Arthur Graham, who lived next door to us in Carlisle used to play at war. We used broomsticks as rifles, and we'd thought of it as a kind of game, until we started to see the wounded soldiers coming home. Some of them were missing legs or arms. Some were blind. Lots had been gassed, like my dad. Dad had managed to get back to the front, but some of these other soldiers couldn't walk more than a few steps without passing out. Arthur and I stopped playing at war after that.

The lorry bounced along the track a bit further, with all of us in the back keeping silent after Sergeant Blake had shouted at Bob, and then it pulled to a halt. We heard the doors at the front open and slam, then Sergeant Blake was standing at the back of the lorry.

"All out!" he said.

We were in a clearing that had a railway track running through it. In the middle of the clearing was a railway carriage made out of polished dark wood. It had brass around the windows and doors, and along the edge of the roof.

"That's a very posh railway carriage," said Nipper.

"But why is it here in the middle of this forest?" asked Bob. "And why are we here with it?"

CHAPTER

"Your first job is to put up the tents," said Sergeant Blake. "They're in the wooden boxes in the lorry."

I spotted a movement in the trees on the other side of the railway track, and then caught a flash of a uniform, before whoever it was disappeared back among the trees.

"There's someone over there, Sergeant," I said. "In those trees."

"French soldiers," said Blake. "Don't worry about them. They're here on special duties as well."

"What special duties, Sarge?" asked Charlie.

"We're guarding this side of the clearing," said Blake.

"But the enemy's a long way away," said Bob. "Right back past the Hindenberg Line."

"You know that for sure, do you, Private Taylor?" snapped Blake. "Our orders are to put a guard line this side of the tracks. The French are doing the same on the other side. You don't talk to them, is that clear?"

"Yes, Sarge," we said.

"Right, start putting up the tents. Then we'll sort out a guard rota."

We unloaded the wooden boxes from the lorry and began setting up our camp.

"There's something funny going on here," said Bob. "Guarding a railway carriage in the middle of a forest? Why? Who's in it?"

"No one, by the look of it," said Nipper. "I've been checking the windows and I haven't spotted anyone inside."

"Well, I'm going to find out," said Bob. "These 'special duties' sound dangerous, and I like to know where the most danger is so I can keep out of it. It's kept me alive so far through this war, and I don't intend anything bad to happen to me now if we're close to the end of it."

"You think we are?" I asked.

"Yes, I do," said Bob. "The Germans have been pushed right back, and thousands have surrendered. We saw it ourselves at Sambre, all those Germans with their hands up. I don't know what's going on here, but it's something unusual. And I'm going to try to find out."

"How?" asked Nipper.

"I bet the French know," said Bob.

"But Sergeant Blake told us not to go and talk to them," I said.

"Who said anything about going to talk to them?" said Bob. "But if I stroll past and one of them asks me for the time, say, or if I think it's going to rain, it would be rude not to answer him. We're allies, after all. And if someone happens to mention this railway carriage. . ."

"Don't say any more," snapped Terry Watts. "That sounds like disobeying orders, and I'm not having any part of it."

"Suit yourself," said Bob, shrugging. "I'd just like to know who or what we're guarding."

As we put the tents up, I had to admit that I was curious about that as well. It had to be important for us to be taken out of the battle. So what was it?

CHAPTER

Much as Bob wanted to talk to the French soldiers and find out what was going on, he never got the chance. Sergeant Blake seemed to know what Bob had in mind and kept a close watch on him. None of the rest of us wanted to get caught, so we kept away from the French soldiers on the other side of the tracks. They must have had the same orders because they kept their distance from us too.

The next day, things started to happen. About the middle of the morning, two large open staff cars pulled up at the French guard line. I was on guard duty on our side of the tracks, along with Bob, Nipper and Charlie. Even from a distance we could see that the chests of the officers in the back of each car were covered in rows of medals, and they all had gold braid on their hats and uniforms. There was a lot of saluting from the French soldiers, and then the two cars drove on. They pulled up beside the railway carriage.

Five of the men got out of the cars and went into the carriage. The two with the most decorations were the ones in the French uniforms. Two others wore the uniforms of the Royal Navy, and the fifth was a British captain.

"This is big," muttered Bob.

"Do you know who they are?" asked Charlie.

"The French ones are Marshal Foch and General Weygand," said Bob.

This news was a big shock for me. Marshal Foch was *the* leader of the Allied forces, the top man in charge of everything: the French and Belgians, the British, the Anzacs, the Canadians, even the Americans. I didn't know who General Weygand was, but he was obviously very important, judging by the array of medals. It meant that something really big was happening here.

"The two Royal Navy men are First Sea Lord Wemyss and Deputy First Sea Lord Hope," said Nipper. "I saw their pictures in the newspaper. They're right at the top too." He shook his head. "I don't know who the captain is, though."

"Stop that chatter!" snapped the voice of Sergeant Blake. "You're on duty!"

The five men stayed inside the railway carriage for the next couple of hours. We were eventually relieved from guard duty by four other blokes. We went back to our tent and sat outside, watching the railway carriage and waiting. What was going on in there?

"They're making a plan," said Bob. "I bet it's about the final attack, or something."

"But why would the top brass from the Royal Navy have anything to do with that?" asked Nipper. "All the fighting's on land, so it's army business."

None of us could answer his question. But that afternoon something happened that gave us a clue.

We heard the rattle of wheels on the railway lines, and then an engine trundled out of the forest, pulling just one carriage behind it. We heard its brakes grinding, and then it stopped behind the stationary carriage in a hissing of steam. As the clouds of steam thinned, we saw Foch, Weygand, Wemyss, Hope and the army captain come out of their carriage and gather at the foot of the steps.

Four men appeared from the newly arrived carriage, walking stiffly down the steps with grim expressions. They headed towards the Allied leaders.

"Germans!" said Bob. "And top Germans as well. Look at the decorations on those uniforms."

Two of the Germans wore army uniforms weighed down with medals and gold braid, and the same went for the one wearing the uniform of the German navy. The fourth man was dressed in civilian clothes, a very smart dark suit and a top hat, of all things.

They stopped in front of the waiting Allied leaders, and then the three in uniform snapped to attention and saluted. Foch didn't return their salute, but the others did. Then all of them walked up the steps and disappeared into the carriage we were guarding.

"Top brass from both sides," muttered Bob. "It's the surrender."

I looked at him, stunned. Could he be right? Could this be the moment the war ended and we could all go home? The thought of it filled me with excitement, going home to see Mam and Dad and Tim and Ann again. But I fought hard not to let myself get too carried away. There'd been so many false hopes, claims that the Germans were beaten and the war was over, but they never turned out to be true.

"If it *is* the surrender, we know why we're here," said Bob. "Us and the French. To protect them. Let's face it, there's a lot of angry people in France who'd like to take their revenge on those Germans in that carriage. That's why there's all this secrecy."

"It's not the surrender," said Nipper, shaking his head. "For that they'd have to have the Kaiser here. The officers couldn't surrender without their leader."

"Maybe he's dead," said Bob. "Some leaders commit suicide when their side loses a war. It's to do with losing their honour."

"That sounds like a stupid thing to do," I said.

"Yeah, well, war's stupid," said Bob. He took a

27

quick look round to check that Sergeant Blake wasn't around to hear him. "Think about it. This has been going on for four years. There's thousands of our lot dead, maybe millions. Same for the Germans. What have we got out of it?"

"We stopped the Germans ruling us," I pointed out.

"Maybe, but will we be any better off when we get back home?"

"We did our duty," said Nipper firmly. "If we hadn't, we'd have ended up as slaves of the Germans."

Bob grimaced. "Sometimes I wonder if it makes any difference to us ordinary people who's in charge at the top," he said. "King or Kaiser. Prime Minister or President. For us folks at the bottom, it always seems to stay the same."

CHAPTER

Whatever was going on with the talks between the top brass clearly wasn't straightforward, because they were in the railway carriage for the next three days. The talks even carried on through the night. Every now and then the Germans would come out and talk privately, before going back inside.

It was on the fourth day of these talks, in the early hours of 11th November, that things changed. I'd got some sleep around midnight, and gone back on guard duty at four o'clock in the morning.

At about half past five in the morning I saw the four Germans come out of the carriage, walking as stiff and straight as when they'd arrived. They climbed back aboard their own carriage. The engine came to life, and I realized that the driver and his crew must have begun firing up the boiler some time before, as if they'd been expecting this. Smoke belched out of the funnel and the engine began to rock, and then the bars along the wheels started moving, and the train went slowly off, taking the Germans away.

The British captain came down the steps of the carriage we were guarding. He signalled to Sergeant Blake and the commander of the French soldiers to come to him. Both marched smartly over and snapped to attention, saluting. The captain returned their salute and said something to them quietly. Then he saluted again, and returned inside the carriage.

Sergeant Blake headed towards us, while the French officer went to his own troops.

"Guard unit, fall in!" commanded Blake.

Me, Bob, Nipper and Charlie formed a line, and were soon joined by the rest of our unit.

"I have been given instructions to alert you to what has occurred here," said Blake. "At five o'clock this morning, an armistice was signed following the surrender of the German forces. This Armistice is to take effect from eleven o'clock today, the eleventh of November 1918, being the eleventh hour of the eleventh day of the eleventh month.

"From that time there will be no more fighting. This message is being sent to all forces. From this moment, the war is over."

CHAPTER

Some of the lads thought this meant we'd be able to get the next boat home to England, but I had my doubts. And I was right. Even though the war was officially over, there was a lot to do. The first thing was to make sure all the Germans' weapons were confiscated, just in case some of them wanted to defy the Armistice. Then the Germans in France and Belgium had to be returned to their own country under guard.

Luckily, it was decided that the French and Belgians should be the ones to oversee the German soldiers being returned to Germany, and then reinforcing the border to make sure they didn't come back. But it still meant it was a few weeks after the Armistice before the 2nd Battalion of the Manchester Regiment was stood down and we really could go home.

Lorries took us back to Calais, where we were put on a troopship bound for Dover. Halfway across the English Channel, I made my way up on deck, because I wanted to see the famous white cliffs as we neared land. I wasn't the only one. After so long away, it seemed like every other soldier had the same idea. Soon the whole deck was filled with men standing looking at the white cliffs as they emerged from a haze. I saw tears in the eyes of more than one tough-looking soldier at the sight.

Standing on English soil again seemed strange. I was home, but part of me still felt like I was back in France, fighting the war. Now I was really back, it struck me that there had been many times when I thought I'd never get home again. But here I was. I'd made it.

Once we were all off the ship, I was officially demobbed and given a travel voucher for the long journey home to use on trains and buses. Some of the other soldiers exchanged their uniform for clean clothes. Bob and I didn't want to hang around in the queue – we were too anxious to get home. Besides, I didn't really mind wearing my uniform. It made me feel proud.

As we came down the gangway from the boat, crowds of men, women and children began cheering and waving at us, There were people lining the route all the way from the disembarkation sheds, and right up to the railway platforms at Dover station. Many of them wanted to shake our hands, and one woman even gave me a bunch of flowers. There were handmade signs being held up as well, greeting us with messages like 'Welcome our heroes' and 'We'll be grateful to you for ever'.

We got on a train from Dover to London. Some of the men were planning on spending a few days in London because it had been a long time since they'd had any proper fun. They wouldn't be able to have much once they got home to their families and had to find work again. Bob and I, though, wanted to keep heading north. Both of us wanted to get home to our families as soon as we could: me to Mam and Dad and my brother and sister, Bob to his wife and son.

When we got to Euston station, we were puzzled to see that a lot of people were wearing cloth masks over their mouths and noses. At Dover there had been a couple of people with scarves pulled up over their mouths too. I'd guessed it was because they were just wrapping up from the icy December weather. Some men whose faces had been badly injured in the war wore masks to hide their wounds, especially if the injury was something really bad. But at Euston it wasn't just men wearing these masks. It was women and children as well. We saw a woman in a very expensive coat, accompanied by a porter wheeling a trolley with loads of luggage, both wearing masks. An elderly gentleman was also wearing one, and from the look of him there was no chance he was a wounded ex-soldier.

"What do you reckon the masks are for?" I asked.

"Gas?" suggested Bob. When we were in the trenches a gas attack had been one of our worst nightmares.

"I don't think so," I said. "Not everyone's wearing them. It's strange."

"I'm going to find out," said Bob. And he headed towards the porter with the mask on.

"'Scuse me!" he called. "Me and my pal have just come back from France, and we're curious about these masks you and others are wearing. What are they for?"

"'Cause of the flu," said the porter.

Bob frowned.

"But everyone gets flu this time of year," he said. "A few days of coughing and sneezing and you get over it. Unless it turns into pneumonia or something bad."

"Not this flu," said the porter. "It's the worst kind there's ever been. They're calling it the Spanish flu 'cause they think it came from Spain."

"How did it get here?" I asked.

"Some say it's the troops coming back home who are bringing it. They reckon after it started in Spain it spread to France." He looked at us suspiciously. "You two are feeling all right, are you?"

"Of course we are," said Bob. "And this is the first we've heard of it."

"How bad is it?" I asked.

"Very bad," said the porter. "People have been

dying from it. And quick too. One day they catch it, a couple of days later they're dead. That's why people are putting masks on, to stop breathing in germs."

"So why isn't everyone wearing them?" asked Bob.

The porter shrugged again.

"Some people think it ain't that serious and it won't happen to them."

As we headed for our train, Bob looked thoughtful.

"If it was in France, how come we didn't hear about it?" he asked.

"Maybe 'cause we were mainly in the north of the country," I said. "Spain's south of France."

Bob nodded. "Maybe," he said.

The journey north was a long one, with several train changes on the way, so we ended up spending a lot of time sitting on cold platforms waiting for trains. At Crewe we were heading in different directions, Bob was getting a train to Manchester and I was heading further north to Carlisle.

"Well, Joe," said Bob. "After all we've been through, it looks like this is goodbye. At least for now."

"If you're ever coming to Carlisle, make sure you

let me know and we'll meet up," I said. We'd already swapped addresses on the train.

"And the same goes for you, if you're ever in Manchester," said Bob. "You'll always be welcome. We can always fit you in." Then, with a grin, he couldn't resist asking me one more time, "How old are you exactly?"

This time I just grinned back and said, "Old enough."

With that, we shook hands and wished one another well, and that was it. The end of my life in the army.

The final part of the train journey to Carlisle seemed to take for ever, with the train crawling up the inclines as it went through and over the high fells of Cumberland and Westmoreland. The haul up to the high point at Shap took so long I thought the train was going to pull to a stop and then roll backwards. But eventually we pulled into Carlisle Citadel station.

Our house was on a terrace in Tait Street, not far from the station. With my kitbag over my shoulder, and the steel of my army boots ringing on the pavement, I made my way home. Perhaps it was because I'd spent so much time out in the open in France, but the houses seemed very small.

When I reached our street, Mr and Mrs Chapel were sitting outside their house on kitchen chairs, just as they had been on the day I left, only now they were bundled up in their winter coats. He was reading a newspaper and she was doing her knitting. Like everyone else on our street, their house was tiny, and the Chapel family had even more of a crush than most. With their kids and relatives there were twelve people to find space for, so the front step made an extra room, if it wasn't too cold out. Of course, it also let them keep an eye on what was going on.

Mrs Chapel looked up as I reached them, and dropped her knitting into her lap.

"Joe Henry!" exclaimed Mr Chapel. "What's happened to you? You look all grown up."

"I've been to war," I said.

Mr Chapel nodded.

"Aye, we heard as much," he said.

Mrs Chapel gave me a stern look.

"Running off and leaving your mother like that," she said. "You should have thought of her."

"I thought of her the whole time I was away," I said.

She didn't say anything to that, and nor did Mr Chapel, but I felt their eyes on me as I approached our front door. As always, I knew it would be unlocked. I stood there for a moment, my hand on the door, wondering what Mam would say when she saw me. Would she be angry? She deserved to be. Still, it was too late to worry about that now. It was time to face her.

I pushed the door open.

"Mam?" I called out. "I'm home!"

CHAPTER

Tim came running down the passage towards me.

"It's Joe! Joe's home!"

Then Ann appeared, looking taller than when I went away. She ran to me and hugged my legs tightly.

"Joe!" she yelled. "It's Joe!"

Mam came out from the back room and stared. She ran forwards and threw her arms around me.

"Joe," she said. "Joe. You've come back."

I felt wet on my cheeks, and realized she was crying.

"It's all right, Mam," I said. "I'm all right."

She pushed away from me and wiped her eyes.

"Why didn't you write and say you were coming?" she asked. "I could have got myself ready!"

"I didn't know if the letter would get here before me," I told her. Then I put my arms around her again and pulled her to me. "I'm sorry I went off the way I did."

She took a deep, steadying breath.

"You're home again, that's the main thing," she said.

As I held her tight, I asked, "Have you heard anything about Dad?"

"He's here," she said. And she called out, "Walter! Joe's home!"

I let her go and turned to look towards the back kitchen. Dad was standing in the doorway.

But this was a different Dad from the one who'd gone away to war last. He was bent over and thin, leaning heavily on a walking stick. He didn't move, he just stood there, glaring at me.

"What are you doing here?" he demanded.

I shivered when I heard the anger in his voice.

"I've come home," I said.

Dad leaned on his stick and scowled. The silence seemed to go on and on.

"I don't know how you've got the nerve to show your face here," he said eventually.

I could tell from the way his fists were clenched that it was as much as he could do to stop himself from going for me. In fact, I felt that if he hadn't been leaning so heavily on his walking stick, he would have.

"But … but, Dad…" I protested.

I thought he'd be glad to see me back home, and alive.

"It was bad enough that your mother didn't have me at home to look after her and the children. But I *had* to go and fight, you *chose* to abandon them. You ran away."

"I went to fight to help get you home!" I said.

He shook his head.

"You're not welcome here," he said. "You ran away. Well, you can keep running."

He turned and limped back into the back kitchen.

"Walter!" Mam called after him. "He's our son! And he's back, and alive!"

My heart went out to her as I saw the torment she was in, torn between being glad to see me, and needing to be loyal to Dad.

She turned to me. "He's just upset, Joe. He doesn't mean it. I'll have a word with him. You take Tim and Ann into the parlour." She went to go after Dad, then stopped. "But don't make a mess in there. Take those boots off first."

She disappeared into the back kitchen.

Tim and Ann looked at me, as puzzled as I was at Dad's anger. I unlaced my big heavy boots and put them by the front door.

"Come on," I said. "We'll do what Mam says."

The parlour was shiny clean, as always. It was a room we hardly ever used. It was kept for special occasions, like Christmas, or if someone important came to call – which happened very rarely. But, just in case, it was kept dusted and the small table and sideboard polished. A pair of tiny dogs made of plaster sat next to a small music box on the sideboard, and on the wall hung small framed photos of my nan and grandpa, and Mam and Dad on their wedding day, next to a painting of the Cumbrian countryside.

Tim and Ann sat together on one of the armchairs. I remained standing up; I didn't want to make anything dirty with my uniform. We could just hear Mam and Dad talking in the back kitchen. Mam was doing most of the talking in a low voice, and Dad barked out a couple of angry words every now and then.

"How have you been?" I asked my brother.

"All right," said Tim. "I'm in Mrs Potter's class at school now."

I nodded.

"She's a good teacher," I said. "She was my teacher when I was at Long Street."

"I can do my numbers up to twenty and most of my letters."

"That's good," I said.

Ann didn't say anything, she just sat squashed up next to Tim and looked at me as if she'd never seen me before. In a way she hadn't. She'd never seen me in uniform before, and it was about six months since I'd last been here. For a four-year-old, that's a long time.

"Did you get wounded?" asked Tim. "In the war?"

"Not really," said. "I got hurt a few times, but just cuts and bruises, nothing bad."

"Dad got wounded," said Tim. "In the leg."

"Yes, so I see," I said.

"He can't walk very well," added Tim.

Mam came in. I looked at her enquiringly, but she ignored me. I guessed Dad was still in the same bad mood.

"Let's get you settled back in," she said. "Take your stuff up to your room. Your bed's made up same as always."

"I've been sleeping in it while you've been away," said Tim.

"Ann's been ill quite a lot," said Mam. "She gets restless and kicks, and she kept waking Tim up."

"What's been up with her?" I asked.

Mam hesitated, then said, "Kiddie illnesses mostly. But she had a bad touch of bronchitis a couple of weeks ago."

"I had a fever," said Ann, looking at me, still slightly awed and overcome.

"Are you better now?" I asked.

Ann nodded, but then she gave a cough, a deep-down bronchitis cough that made her bend over double and I thought she was going to fall off the chair.

Mam produced a handkerchief and held it to her mouth.

"Spit it up, love," she said.

Ann coughed again, and this time she spat some phlegm into the handkerchief.

"Good girl," said Mam. She forced a smile at me. "She's getting better," she said.

Whether she was saying it to reassure me or Ann, I wasn't sure.

"Tim can keep the bed," I said. "I'll sleep on the floor. I've slept on worse while I was at the war."

Mam shook her head. "It's your bed, and I told Tim he could only sleep in it until you came home. I knew you'd come home, despite what your dad says."

"I went to try and get the war won so Dad could come home quicker," I said again.

"I know." Mam nodded. "But . . . it was the way you did it that upset your dad. Going off without a word. Lying about your age."

"I had to lie about my age otherwise the army wouldn't have let me join," I said. "Lots of others did the same."

"The thing is, you're back," said Mam, smiling.

"And I'm happy on the mattress, honestly. Let Tim keep the bed, he's a big lad now." I ruffled my little brother's hair and he grinned at me.

"What happened to Dad's leg?" I asked, glancing up at Mam.

Mam hesitated, an unhappy look on her face, and I kicked myself for asking, because I realized it upset her to talk about it.

"They said he was lucky," she said. "It was a machine gun. They thought he'd lose his leg, but he didn't. Others did. Ted Payne in Edward Street lost both of his, poor man. He pushes himself around the streets now on a kid's pram."

She hesitated, then added, "He came back in September. He was in hospital for six weeks before they let him come home."

"I'm sorry," I said. "About Dad getting wounded, and for going off the way I did. But I did it for good reasons." It seemed a bit silly now, to think that I had believed I could make a difference to how quickly the war ended.

"I know you did, Joe. But it'll take a while before your dad sees it that way."

CHAPTER

I took my kitbag upstairs to my room – mine and Tim's room, now – and dropped it down beside the bed, my mind in a whirl. My homecoming was so different from how I'd thought it would be. All the time I'd been away, I'd been thinking about Dad and wondering where he was. I had prayed that he'd survive the war and that I would see him again. Now I had seen him, and he wasn't too keen on seeing me.

Dad had always been a big, strong man. He could pick me up with one arm and Tim with the other, even when I was getting big. He'd looked bad when he came home from the war that first time, after being gassed, but he was still in fairly good shape when he went back. But now ... now he looked like an old man.

I heard a knock at the front door, and voices, and then Mam called up to me.

"Joe, it's Arthur come to see you."

Arthur! I hoped my best pal would be glad to see me back at least. I hurried downstairs and saw Arthur grinning at me.

"Hello, Joe!" he said.

"Hang on while I put my boots on," I said.

"Aren't you going to change out of your army stuff?" asked Mam.

"Later," I said. "I don't know if my old clothes will still fit me."

Even though I had more muscles, I'd lost weight because of the limited rations. Besides, Arthur's arrival had given me a good opportunity to escape from the house and Dad's bad mood.

I laced up my boots and joined Arthur out in the street.

"Let's go to the park," I said. "Things are a bit topsy-turvy indoors."

"Your dad, eh?" said Arthur.

"You know?" I said.

"He's been ranting about you since he got back from hospital," said Arthur. "He was pretty upset when he found out you'd gone off the way you did."

"He still is," I said.

We headed for Victoria Park just a few streets away in the city centre.

"Are you still working for the Parks Department?" I asked.

Arthur nodded. "Yes."

All of us – except the rich – left school at thirteen and went to work. Because I'd been in my last year of school before I went off to war, I hadn't got any kind of job fixed up for when I left.

"Any chance of me getting a job with you?" I asked. "Now I'm back I've got to find some work."

"I doubt it," replied Arthur. "It's the wrong time of year for planting flowers. Mostly we're doing work on old trees."

"I can do that," I said. "We sawed down a lot

of trees in Flanders. We used 'em as props in the trenches, and to get fires going."

He shook his head.

"They're cutting back on the number of people they take on," he said. "There's not enough money to pay people after the war."

We reached Victoria Park and he gestured at the empty flower beds. "Spring'll be the next big planting."

We sat down on one of the benches.

"What about the railway? There's always lots of work there, track-laying and such," Arthur suggested. "What about being a track layer, like your dad was before the war? Maybe he could get you in."

I shook my head.

"Dad isn't talking to me, so I'm pretty sure he won't give me any help that way."

"He'll settle down now you're back," said Arthur. "You'll see."

We were quiet for a moment, just watching the people wandering around the park. I felt like I wasn't quite there, like I might wake up any minute and be back in the trenches.

"What was it like?" asked Arthur.

"Horrible," I said.

"After you left, I tried to join up as well," said Arthur. "I did what you did, I went to the Lonsdales and told them I was eighteen, and they signed me up and sent me to the training camp." He sighed. "Trouble was, Mam turned up with my birth certificate and showed it to the officer in charge, and when he saw that I was fourteen he sent me home." He shuddered. "Being brought home by my mam like a naughty schoolboy – I've never been so embarrassed. I've been ashamed of it ever since."

"Don't blame your mam," I said. "She was only doing what she thought was right, to save you."

"Yes, but you went!" said Arthur. "And you came home!"

"I was one of the lucky ones," I told him. "Most of the underage lads who went never made it back. A lot of them went to pieces when they found out what it was really like going into battle, with real bullets being fired at you and the blokes around you getting shot to bits and dying. And some of them were too much the other way, so set on proving they were tough they ran straight into the bullets."

"How did you survive?" asked Arthur.

"Luck. And we had a good officer leading us who did his best not to take chances. He followed orders all right when we had to go over the top, but he showed us how to zigzag and keep low to stop the Hun from getting a good aim at us." I sighed. "Not that it did him much good. He got shot dead in the last battle we were in."

I suddenly noticed an elderly woman a few yards away, watching me. I didn't recognize her. I was just wondering if she was the gran of one of my friends at school when she came towards our bench. My heart began to beat a little faster, and I straightened up. If I was expected to recognize her, and didn't, it was bound to get back to Mam and Dad.

"Soldier?" she said.

I immediately stood up, as did Arthur.

"Yes, ma'am," I said, very respectful.

"You're back from the war, then?"

"Yes, ma'am. Just got back today."

She nodded.

"You did a brave thing," she said. She hesitated, wringing her hands together. "Your family are lucky you came home. My two sons and their sons all died out there in Flanders, all four of them." She nodded again, her eyes glistening. "This country should be grateful to you. And them."

"Yes, ma'am. Thank you, ma'am," I said.

I didn't know what else to say. She turned and shuffled away.

"See," said Arthur as I sat back down. "You're a hero."

CHAPTER

Despite what Arthur said, Dad didn't settle down. He glared at me when I came into the back kitchen and things didn't get better over the next few days,

He sat by the coal-fired range, day in, day out, in his high-backed wooden armchair, reading and re-reading his newspaper, and ignoring me except for a grim glare when I tried to make conversation with him.

It was worst during the day because there was just me and him in the house. Mam had recently got herself a part-time job at Mrs Wilson's drapery shop, after being laid off from the munitions factory. Tim was at school, and Ann went to Mrs Carson's four doors down the street, who looked after her while Mam was at work. Ann had first started going to Mrs Carson's when Mam got the job at the munitions place during the war. Mrs Carson had two kids of her own and took in other kids during the day so their mothers could work. It cost Mam a couple of shillings a week, but she said it was worth it.

"It means I can still bring in money, although not as much as I did at the munitions factory," Mam told me, two days after I'd got back. "I know it upsets your dad that I go out to work, but that's the way it is. We have to do what we have to do."

She and I were walking through the town centre. Mam had gone out to do some shopping, and I offered to carry the bags for her. The truth is, it gave me an excuse to get out of the house.

"Why did you decide to leave the munitions place?" I asked.

"I didn't decide to leave it," said Mam. "When the war ended they said they weren't going to need that many bombs and bullets any more, so they laid us off. The twelve thousand women who were working there, that is. Most of the five thousand men stayed on.

"The trouble is, with the men back from the war they don't want us women doing what they think of as men's work any more. They needed us because the men were away, but now. . ." She shook her head. "Still, in a way it's better. The money was good, but it meant getting the train to Eastriggs. At least I'm here for picking up Ann, so she doesn't have to stay so long at Mrs Carson's."

"Dad's still not talking to me," I told her gloomily. "I try and talk to him, but he just grunts."

"He's upset because he can't find work," said Mam. "He went for jobs, but they saw him limping the way he does and told him they hadn't got anything for him."

"What about the railway?" I suggested. "Surely they'll take him back."

"That was the first place he tried when he came out of the infirmary," said Mam. "They told him he couldn't be a track layer any more, not with his leg. He told them he wasn't suffering and insisted he was as strong as ever, but they said no, they needed men who were fully fit." She sighed. "It was the same story wherever he tried."

"How about office work?" I said. "Dad can read and write."

She shook her head.

"He couldn't stand being in an office," she said. "He likes being outside."

"Well, he's not outside now," I said. "He's stuck in the back kitchen every day."

"He'll come up with something," she said. "He's worried, you see, about us being turned out of the house if we can't pay the rent. I tell him that my money from Mrs Wilson's will take care of it."

"And I'll get a job, Mam," I assured her. "I promise you. I'm out every day looking."

"I know you are, Joe," said Mam.

I'd called at several places around the town, from shops to timber yards, asking if they needed any help, although it was as much to get me out of the house during the day. So far I'd had no luck – there just didn't seem to be enough work. But on the third day of looking, my luck changed. They were mending the main road that goes from Carlisle to Newcastle, and they needed labourers to break up the old damaged bits of road before they could put the new road surface down. Even better, they wanted me to start straight away.

The next morning, I arrived at the site, met the other blokes and quickly got to grips with the work. It was hard going, but I'd got used to it digging trenches in Flanders. It felt good to be doing something again.

The evening of my first day at work, Mam made a special supper of lamb with roast potatoes. It was meant to be a celebration, but Dad's silence sagged over us. The happiness I felt about my job started to ebb away.

"So how was it today, Joe?" Mam asked, trying to lighten the mood.

"Good. I started work on the Newcastle road, at the Carlisle end," I said. "We're breaking up the old cobbles so they can put down a new road surface."

"I'm so pleased they took you on," said Mam. "Isn't it good, Walter?"

Dad just gave a kind of grunt and carried on eating his supper.

I wished that Dad could have done a full day's hard work too. I could tell he missed feeling useful – it couldn't be making him feel any better that I'd managed to find a job when he hadn't. An idea popped into my head.

"I wondered, Dad, if you wanted me to have a word with the gang foreman? It's George Potts, who used to live in Caldew Street. I could put in a word for you with him."

It was as if I'd slapped him. He stared at me and I could see a red flush of anger rising across his face. He threw down his knife and fork on the table.

"*You*. Put in a word for *me*? A *kid* putting in a word for his father?"

Quickly, Mam said, "Now, Walter, I'm sure Joe didn't mean anything bad by it—"

"I'm the man in this house!" he raged. "If there's any word to be put in, it should be me doing it, not you!"

He jerked up, almost knocking his chair over, and stormed out of the kitchen. A few seconds later we heard the front door slam.

"I was only trying to help!" I said.

"Your dad's a very proud man," said Mam sadly. She looked at Tim and Ann who were sitting, looking at her wide-eyed, their supper forgotten.

"Is Dad coming back?" asked Tim, on the point of tears.

"Of course he is," said Mam. "He's just gone out to blow his temper off. He'll be back very soon. Now eat your supper."

CHAPTER

I was tired after my first day of work, and the mattress Mam had put on the floor was comfortable, but I couldn't sleep. I kept thinking about how to make things better with Dad, for everyone's sake. It was driving me mad, and it wasn't doing anyone else in the house any good. I had to do something about it, but the only answer to the problem seemed that I'd have to leave home. But where would I go? I could write to Eric or Billy in Manchester, but going that far away would upset Mam, Tim and Ann all over again.

In the next room, Ann started coughing, that same horrible bronchitis cough. I heard her thrashing about, and then Mam's footsteps on the landing.

"There, there," she said. "It's all right. Mam's here."

Ann's coughs grew quieter, and finally I managed to drop off to sleep.

I was up early the next morning to get to work. The road gang started at half past seven, even though it was still dark. Before I set off, I knocked on Arthur's door. I knew he didn't start work until eight.

He was eating a piece of bread when he opened the door.

"Joe," he said, swallowing his mouthful. "What's wrong?"

I told him about what had happened at supper.

"It can't go on, Arthur," I said. I looked at my shoes, embarrassed. "I was wondering if I could come and stay with you for a couple of days, just until things blow over."

"I'll ask my mam," said Arthur. "But I'm sure she'll say it's all right. She's out at the moment on one of her cleaning jobs."

"Thanks, Arthur," I said. "I'll pop in after work to see what she says."

Arthur's mam, Mary Graham, is a widow. Arthur's dad died when Arthur was just six, so Mrs Graham went to work cleaning houses, to keep money coming in. Arthur started doing odd jobs – unpacking stock in shops and tidying up people's gardens – from when he was seven, to make sure they had money to pay the rent and eat.

When the munitions factory at Eastriggs opened in 1916, Mrs Graham went to work there, the same as Mam did, but now the war was over, she'd been laid off, like Mam and the other women, which is why she was back cleaning.

I spent the day with the road gang, breaking up the road and throwing the old cobbles on the back of a lorry. It was physically exhausting, but I didn't mind. At least no one was shooting at us.

As it was Friday, in the afternoon I could collect my wages for my first two days' work. Arthur must have been watching out for me, because his door opened as I neared our house.

"Mam says it's all right for you to stay," he told me.

"She'll put down a mattress on the floor in my room for you."

"Thanks, Arthur," I said.

I felt a rush of relief and then a surge of guilt. Mam was going to be so upset.

"When do you want to come? She says you can move in tonight."

"Tomorrow," I said. "I need to tell everyone first."

"Your dad should be pleased," said Arthur.

"Yes, but Mam and the kids won't," I said.

CHAPTER

It was strange. I'd run into machine-gun fire. I'd climbed over barbed wire with soldiers dying next to me. I'd crouched for hours in trenches, listening to shells exploding all around me. But the thought of telling Mam I was moving in with Arthur made me more nervous than anything I'd faced at the front.

The first thing I did was give Mam a little money towards the rent from my wage packet along with a few pennies for Tim and Ann for sweets. I would have given her more, but I knew I'd need some to pay Mrs Graham for my keep.

Mam had made a stew for us, and we ate it in silence, mainly because Dad glowered at anyone who opened their mouth to speak.

After we'd finished eating, I knew I couldn't put off telling them any longer.

"I was thinking. . ." I started to say, trailing off as my courage failed me.

Mam looked at me, curious. There was nothing for it but to say it straight out.

"I thought I'd stay next door with Arthur for a while," I said, trying to sound casual about it, though my heart was beating hard. "They've got more room."

Mam and Dad looked at one another, Mam concerned, Dad grim-faced.

"Are you sure it'll be all right with Mrs Graham?" asked Mam.

"Arthur said it would," I said.

"So you talked to her first before you talked to us, did you?" said Dad.

"Only to check," I said. It was like I couldn't win –

Dad was angry at me for being around at home, and angry at me when I tried to leave.

He gave a grunt, pushed himself up from the table and limped out of the room leaning heavily on his stick. I heard him go into the parlour.

I looked at Mam apologetically.

"I'm sorry, Mam," I said. "But it's not good for anyone, the way it's been here since I came back."

"He'll get better," said Mam quietly.

She got up and went after Dad. Tim and Ann were staring at me.

"Will you come back?" asked Tim. "Or will it be like before? You went out and never came back."

"I sent Mam a postcard," I said.

"That didn't come for ages," said Tim.

"She cried when it came," said Ann.

"And she cried at night for weeks," said Tim. "When we were in bed. We heard her."

"I'm only going to be next door at Arthur's," I said.

But Tim and Ann just looked at me.

CHAPTER

The next morning, I packed my kitbag and went downstairs to tell Mam and Dad I was off.

"Your dad's gone out," said Mam. "He said he had to see someone."

I felt sure he'd just made up an excuse so he didn't have to be there when I left. I didn't say that to Mam. I didn't want to upset her.

"Just remember, I'm only next door at Arthur's if you need me for anything," I reminded her.

She gave me a hug. I shook hands with Tim and

gave Ann a cuddle, and then left. I had said it was only going to be for a short time, but I knew – and I think so did Mam – that I wouldn't come home again until Dad and I found a way to get along. If we ever did.

I'd been a boy when I left home to go to war, but all the things that had happened to me while I was away had made me a man, and I couldn't stay at home with Dad giving me orders like I was still a little child. Especially when I felt he was being unfair.

Arthur's mam greeted me with a big smile.

"Welcome, Joe!" she said. "Have you had breakfast?"

"I have, thank you, Mrs Graham," I said.

"You just make yourself at home."

"I will," I said. "It's only until things get sorted out at ours, and if they don't, I'll look for a room somewhere, I promise."

"No you won't, Joe Henry," she said sternly. "You stay here as long as you want. I'm sure your dad will come round." She took her coat from the peg and began to put it on. "Anyway, you two can look after yourselves for a bit. I'm off to the town hall for the demonstration."

"What demonstration?" I asked.

"Votes for women," said Mrs Graham.

"Oh, Mam," groaned Arthur. "People might see you!"

"I hope they do," said Mrs Graham. "It's about time we ordinary women got the right to say who we want in charge of us. We were necessary when there was a war on, but as soon as it's finished we're thrown over. It's not right."

"But women have got the vote, Mam," said Arthur. "I saw it in the paper in February."

"Only if they're over thirty and they own a house. So it's only rich women who get the vote. What about the rest of us? We're the ones who do the hard work. And why do we have to be thirty? Men can vote when they're twenty-one *and* they get the vote whether they own a house or not. Is that fair?" She opened the door. "Look after your gran while I'm out. She could do with some fresh air."

"I hope she's not going to be waving a banner," said Arthur as she left. "Everyone will see her."

Arthur and I played a couple of games of draughts, like we used to do in the old days, and then we got ready to take his gran out. We set up her wheelchair –

which wasn't really a proper wheelchair but an old folding pushchair – and then helped her put on her coat and shoes.

"It's too cold to go out," she complained, scowling.

"You'll enjoy it once you're out, Gran," said Arthur.

She continued to grumble at us as we helped her into her wheelchair. Arthur's gran was his late father's mother, and very different from his mam. Her face was shrivelled like a tortoise's, and her scowl could curdle milk, but her sharp eyes saw everything. I wondered if Dad would end up like her when he got older – scowling and suspicious.

Me and Arthur took turns pushing the wheelchair. At first we took her to Victoria Park, but Arthur's gran said the wind was too icy and there was nothing interesting to see, so we headed towards the town centre where it would be more sheltered.

It was a Saturday and nearing Christmas, so the town centre was busy with shoppers. We kept being stopped by friends of Arthur's gran, so it took us a while to get to the main square by the town hall.

A group of women were standing on the steps of the tall cross opposite the town hall. They were holding up placards that said 'Votes for ALL Women', and it looked as if one of the women was giving a speech. I spotted Mrs Graham near the steps of the cross, and nudged Arthur, who groaned.

"At least she hasn't got a banner," he muttered.

Just then, the crowd burst into applause at whatever the speaker had said.

"What does suffrage mean?" I asked.

"I don't know," said Arthur. "It's something to do with voting."

"A bunch of fools," said Arthur's gran with a snort. "What do they want the vote for?"

"Quite right, Ma," said a big, rough-looking man standing next to us. Then he shouted at the crowd, "You already have the vote! Why are you still complaining?"

"You women don't deserve to vote if you're going to act like a bunch of yowling cats," shouted another man.

He strode forward and grabbed the placard that one of the women was holding and tried to take it off her. She resisted, holding on to it tightly, and there was a tussle between them. Other men moved forwards to do the same, and grab the banners and placards, and the women resisted. I saw a woman bash one of them on the head with her placard.

"This is getting ugly," muttered Arthur. "You look after Gran, I'm going to help Mam!"

But before he could, there was the shrill sound of a police whistle, and suddenly the square was full of policemen. I realized they'd been waiting nearby the side of the town hall in case trouble started.

As soon as the police appeared the men vanished back into the crowd, or slipped down side streets, but it soon became obvious that it wasn't the men the police were after. The police arrested several of the women demonstrators on the steps of the cross, including the one who'd been making the speech, and bundled them into a black police van. It was very unfair. Why weren't they arresting the men who'd tried to grab the banners? After all, they'd started the trouble. Some of the other women tried to stop them taking her away, but the police simply took them as well, putting them in the police van.

"Let's get away from here," I said. "I think your mam's gone."

I couldn't spot her in the square any more.

Hopefully she had slipped away, rather than been arrested.

"Good idea," said Arthur.

We turned his gran's wheelchair around and pushed her away from the square.

"Huh, just as it was getting interesting," she grumbled.

It took us a while to get back to Tait Street. Every time Arthur's gran saw someone she knew, she stopped to talk about the trouble at the demonstration and the arrests.

"What's the point of women voting?" said one old man. "They don't know anything about politics. They don't even care!"

"The ones in the square seemed to," I said. "Why shouldn't women have a vote?"

The old man glared at me.

"You kids don't understand the way things work," he said. "Wait 'til you get out in the real world."

I opened my mouth to say that I had been out in the real world, that I had fought in the war. But the way Arthur's gran was scowling at me made me close my mouth again. I'd already upset Dad enough to make it impossible to live at home, I didn't want the same thing to happen with Arthur's gran.

When we finally got back to Tait Street, we found Arthur's mam had beaten us home and was sitting at the table with a cup of tea, calm as anything.

"Are you all right?" I asked. "We saw the trouble in the square."

"It was all going well until some stupid men tried to take our banners," said Mrs Graham. "It was exactly as they treated us in 1913. As if the war changed nothing!"

"Votes for women," said Arthur's gran with a snort. "Lot of nonsense. Why do women want to get involved in voting? Leave it to the men, that's what I say. Women have got enough to do with cooking and cleaning and looking after the house. We never had time to think about voting when I was young."

"Things were different in your day, Meg," said Mrs Graham.

CHAPTER

That evening, we sat by the fire in the kitchen range. Gran had nodded off in her chair, Arthur was reading a book and Mrs Graham was knitting. I was looking into the hot coals, watching as the flames curled round and flickered. I wondered how many times I'd crouched in the cold and soaking wet of the trenches, wishing I could be beside a fire like this.

"I'm glad the war's over," said Mrs Graham suddenly, her voice breaking into my thoughts.

"So is everyone," I said.

"Eastriggs was a terrible place to work," she said. "The money was good, but the work was horrible."

"Mum never said much about her work," I said.

"They told us not to talk about it because important war work should be kept secret." She gave a mocking laugh. "Secret? Eastriggs was the biggest munitions factory in the whole world. Everyone knew what we were making. The truth was, they didn't want anyone to know how dangerous it was to work there."

"What do you mean?" I asked.

"People got blown up," she said in a quiet voice. "We used to make eight hundred tons of cordite a week, for making bombs and putting in bullets. We used to mix nitroglycerine, guncotton and petroleum jelly together and then knead it into a sort of dough. Deadly stuff, nitroglycerine. If you didn't handle it properly it could explode. And if you had to mix it with sulphur, it turned your skin yellow."

That night, as I lay on the mattress on the floor with Arthur snoring just above me, I kept thinking about Eastriggs. Mam had never said much about it. She didn't want to worry me, I suppose. And I had never asked her about it, I was too absorbed in what I was doing, and what was happening at the front.

I had never thought of Mam as fighting a war too.

The next morning, when Mrs Graham took Arthur's gran a cup of tea in bed, she came down and said the old lady was feeling poorly. She was coughing and shivering, and said her head hurt. I wondered if she'd caught bronchitis because of the damp, like Ann.

Mrs Graham made her a drink of hot lemon, which Mam used to make for Ann, but Arthur's gran just seemed to get worse as the day went on. I popped in once to take her some water. Her eyes were closed and she was very hot, sweat rolling down her face. Her skin, usually so pale, looked almost purple.

I told Mrs Graham, who went upstairs at once. She came back down looking worried.

"I think we might have to get Doctor Campbell in," she said.

Doctor Campbell lived in a big house on Warwick Road. How he could afford such a nice home, I didn't know. Normally, doctors were expensive but Doctor

Campbell often treated people he knew would never be able to pay.

Mrs Graham went off to get Doctor Campbell, leaving Arthur and me to watch over her. We sat together in her room. Her eyes were closed as if she was asleep, but she kept shivering and coughing. She never answered us when we spoke to her.

Mrs Graham was back quickly.

"Doctor Campbell's out on a call," she said. "His housekeeper says lots of people have been calling for him with the same symptoms. She'll ask him to visit us as soon as he gets back."

We took turns to go up to see how she was, and if she wanted anything, while we waited for the doctor. Each time she didn't answer, just lay there, making a terrible wheezing sound.

In the middle of the afternoon I left Arthur and his mam in the living room and went up to check on Arthur's gran. She lay on her back, her eyes closed and her mouth open, but the wheezing sound had stopped.

I put my ear to her mouth, then took a small mirror for the dresser and held it to her lips. No steam formed on the glass. She wasn't breathing.

I ran downstairs.

"Mrs Graham, I think. . . I-I think she's . . . dead."

Mrs Graham raced back up the stairs, Arthur and I just behind her. She felt for a pulse and nodded.

"Poor Meg," she said.

She blinked, then wiped away a tear, then turned and told us, "You two go downstairs. I'll look after her."

Arthur followed me down the stairs.

"It was so quick," he said in a stunned voice. "She was all right last night."

Just then, there was a knock at the door. I opened it and saw Doctor Campbell, who gave me a tired smile.

"Mrs Graham left a message," he said.

"It's Arthur's gran," I said. "She was ill, but now she's . . . well, she's died."

"Where is she?" he asked.

"Upstairs."

He sighed and his shoulders slumped, as if there was an invisible kitbag weighing him down. He headed upstairs. Arthur and I followed, but we didn't go into the room. We waited on the landing and listened.

"It was flu," we heard Doctor Campbell say.

"Flu?" said Mrs Graham. "Flu doesn't kill people that quick."

"This one does," said the doctor. "They're calling it the Spanish flu. It's the most dangerous flu there's ever been. This is the sixth case I've been called to today. I'm sad to say, your mother-in-law is the fourth to die."

The Spanish flu! The same virus the porter told us about at the station.

"You don't have a telephone, do you?" asked the doctor.

"No," said Mrs Graham.

"I'll get my wife to phone the undertakers for you. Will Fishers be all right?"

Mrs Graham mumbled something we couldn't hear.

"After Fishers have taken her, disinfect as much as you can," said Dr Campbell. "Burn the bedding."

Arthur and I went back downstairs as he came out of the bedroom, followed by Mrs Graham.

"I'm afraid I have to go," he said. "I've got more cases to look at, all of them the same. It seems to be an epidemic."

"How much do I owe you, doctor?" asked Mrs Graham, still looking numbed.

"We'll sort that out another time," said Doctor Campbell. "And I'm very sorry, Mrs Graham. There was nothing anyone could have done for her."

CHAPTER

I went next door to tell Mam and Dad the bad news. As I walked through the door I nearly fell over Ann, who was sitting in the passage playing with a rag doll.

"It's Joe!" Ann shouted out, and jumped up and ran to hug my legs.

Mam and Tim appeared from the back kitchen, Mam wiping her hands on a tea towel.

"What's wrong, Joe?" asked Mam, catching sight of my face.

"It's Arthur's gran," I said. "She's just died. The flu."

"Oh no," said Mam, her hand flying to her mouth. "I'd better go and help Mrs Graham."

I shook my head.

"You'd better not," I said. "Doctor Campbell's been and he's told her to disinfect everything and burn the bedding. He says it's very catching. I've just come round to warn you."

"I know there's a lot about," said Mam. "When I was round at Mrs Carson's picking up Ann the other day, she said some of the families had it. I was thinking I'd keep Ann at home for a while, just in case."

"Doctor Campbell says this flu is the most dangerous he's ever seen," I said. I thought back to the people Billy and I had seen wandering around Euston station. "I have an idea. When I was in London on the way home, I saw people wearing masks."

"Masks?" said Tim. "Like robbers?"

"Yes, like robbers," I said, nodding. "But they were wearing the masks to stop breathing in flu germs. They had the flu in London before we did."

"Scarves," said Mam. "We'll wear scarves over our mouths when we go out."

"Or handkerchiefs," I said. "And I know it sounds silly, but soak them in vinegar. When I was in the trenches we used to have masks soaked in vinegar to try and protect us in gas attacks. It might help."

"I will, but I don't know if your dad will wear one. You know how stubborn he can be."

"Where is he?" I asked.

"He's out at the moment," said Mam.

"Where?"

"I think he's gone to see some pal of his at the railway. He's still hoping to get a job there."

I nodded. "I'd better get back next door, Mrs Graham is going to need some help." I turned towards the front door, then stopped. "I'm sorry things are the way they are. I'd better not hug you in case I'm. . ."

"Yes, I know." Mam nodded. "I'll tell your dad about Arthur's gran, and the scarves and vinegar. You take care, son."

It was late in the afternoon before Fishers came to take poor old Mrs Graham away. Then Arthur, Mrs Graham and I set to work to disinfect the house. We took her bedding out into the garden and set fire to it. As we stood beside the flames, I saw black smoke rising up from other gardens. I guessed they'd been given the same instructions.

CHAPTER

I went back to work the next day, but Arthur stayed at home to help his mam.

I'd soaked a big handkerchief in vinegar and tied it round my mouth and nose. When the other blokes saw me, they burst out laughing.

"Look, it's Joe the bank robber!" Andy said, laughing.

"There's no money here," chuckled Bert. "Maybe he's come to rob us of cobbles!"

"It's to try and keep the flu at bay," I told them.

"Flu?" said Andy with a snort. "I've had flu loads of times."

"Not like this," I said. "The doctor says it's the most dangerous he's ever seen. And when I was coming through London on my way back from the front, everyone was wearing masks because the flu was making them drop like flies."

Andy and a couple of the others carried on sniggering, but I just shrugged and started digging. Their attitudes began to change when they realized that a lot of the blokes hadn't turned up for work. In fact, out of the road gang of twenty, only ten of us were there.

Our foreman, George Potts, didn't arrive until nearly nine o'clock.

"I'm sorry I'm late, lads," he said. "I've been going round houses to find out who was going to make it to work today, as a couple of the lads sent word they were ill. Loads of 'em have gone down with this flu." He hesitated, then said unhappily, "In fact, both Mick and Geordie died from it over the weekend."

"Died?" said Andy. "But ... but they're big strong blokes. They were fine on Friday!"

"It turns out it doesn't matter how big and strong you are, it seems this particular flu can kill an ox," said George.

And so, short-handed though we were, we set to work. It was the same as in the war, your mates die but there is still a job to be done. You have to get on with it.

Andy and Bert were the first to tie handkerchiefs around their noses and mouths.

When I got back home after work, Arthur was in the kitchen peeling potatoes. There were sausages frying in the pan on the top of the range.

"Your mam put you in charge of supper?" I asked. Arthur put down the potato he was holding and looked at me grimly.

"She's next door, at your house," he said. "Your dad and Ann have both gone down with the flu."

My stomach dropped. I turned around without another word and rushed next door. I was sick with fear to think of Ann and her bad cough, and Dad with his weak lungs from being gassed. Mrs Graham was in our kitchen with saucepans of water bubbling away on the range. Tim was sitting at the table, looking lost and bewildered.

"Ann and Dad are poorly," he said.

"They're upstairs," Mrs Graham told me. "Your mam's with them. I'm boiling water ready to scald things."

I hurried upstairs. Mam had brought a mattress into her and Dad's room for Ann, and Dad was lying on the bed. Both looked dreadful. They were sweating and making the same wheezing sound that Arthur's gran had made. Mam was wiping a wet rag over Dad's forehead. I saw she'd already put one on Ann's head. A bowl of water was on the floor beside Dad's bed.

"What can I do?" I asked. "Shall I go and get Doctor Campbell?"

"He's been," said Mam. "It's the flu all right."

"They should be in hospital," I said.

"The infirmary's full, they can't take any more. Same for the cottage hospitals. Dr Campbell said we must try to keep them comfortable. He's given me some aspirin, but he's not sure how much good it will do."

I felt sick with fear and panic. This was my fault! I'd brought the flu into the house!

"I did this," I blurted out. "When I came round yesterday, Ann hugged me. I brought it round from the Grahams'."

"No," said Mam firmly, shaking her head. "Ann probably caught it from some of the other kids at Mrs Carson's. It was nothing to do with you. There's so much of it about, we couldn't have stopped it."

She turned back to Dad, and I hovered over her feeling helpless. After what had happened to Arthur's gran, I knew how quickly it could take effect.

"What can I do?" I asked.

"We need to watch them, see if they get worse," said Mam. "Doctor Campbell says we've got to try and bring their fevers down, so I'm keeping them cool with cold-water flannels. And we've got to keep making them drink."

"What about Tim?" I asked.

"Mrs Graham says she'll take him in. So it's down to you and me taking turns to look after them."

I looked at Dad and little Ann. After what had happened to Arthur's gran, I wasn't going to let them out of my sight.

CHAPTER

It was a long night. I remember when I was in France, a doctor at a field hospital telling me that the ill people were always at their worst between one o'clock and three o'clock in the morning. I didn't know if this was true, but I watched Dad and Ann closely, just in case.

We kept them cool with rags dipped in cold water, listening to their dreadful rattling coughs. When they weren't coughing, they were spluttering and wheezing. But at least their faces hadn't gone the terrible purple colour that Arthur's gran's had.

At four o'clock in the morning, Mam patted my hand.

"Go to bed and get some rest," she said. "Your head's nodding."

"I'll be all right," I assured her. "We used to stay awake all night in the trenches."

"We'll need to watch them all day tomorrow," she said. "You'll be no use to me if you fall asleep then. Go and get some rest. I'll wake you in a couple of hours and you can take over."

It made sense, so I went into the other room and lay down on the mattress on the floor. Even though I'd agreed with Mam that I'd rest, I was determined to stay awake in case they took a turn for the worse and she needed me. But the next thing I knew, Mam was shaking me awake.

"Your turn, Joe," she said through a yawn.

"What time is it?" I asked.

"Six o'clock. They're both still the same, no worse, no better."

I got up and Mam flopped down on the mattress.

Both Dad and Ann were still asleep. I checked their foreheads. Ann was hot, but Dad's temperature felt almost normal. I bathed Ann's forehead in cold water, and then went back to Dad. He wasn't sweating like last night, and although he was still wheezing, his coughs didn't have the same dreadful rattling sound.

Dad's eyes flickered.

"Doris," he croaked.

"No, Dad. It's me, Joe."

His eyes opened. He peered at me, then blinked and his eyes closed again.

"Where . . . where's your mam?"

His voice was so thin that I could hardly hear him.

"Asleep," I said. "She was up all night. I took over so she could rest. I'll wake her."

"No," he said.

His voice had more force to it with that one word. He reached out and gripped my arm tightly, his hand bony but strong.

"I . . . got a job," he said.

"A job?"

He swallowed, then forced out the words, "Booking office. Carlisle station."

"Dad, that's brilliant!" I said.

"Haven't . . . told your mam yet. Wanted . . . to

surprise her." He coughed. "Don't know if I'm going to make it, though."

"What do you mean?" I demanded.

"You know."

He coughed again.

"If you're talking about dying, you can forget that," I told him firmly. "The Hun couldn't kill you. You're not going to let a few germs do what they couldn't, are you? You're not going to die here. Me and Mam won't let you."

He coughed again, then spluttered through the saliva that bubbled between his lips, "You're giving me orders now, are you?"

"Yes," I said. "Dad, you've been a hard, stubborn man all your life. Don't go soft on me now."

There was a sudden coughing and moaning from Ann on the mattress. Dad turned his head towards the sound.

"Who's that?"

"Ann," I told him. "She's ill with the flu too."

"She shouldn't be in here," he said.

He tried to sit up, but fell back on his pillow.

"She's in here so we can keep an eye on both of you," I told him.

I knelt down beside Ann. Her eyes were closed, but she was thrashing around in her sleep. I put my hand to her forehead. She was even hotter.

I plunged a rag into the cold water, squeezed it out and wiped it gently over her face and neck. She carried on coughing. Then she opened her eyes and looked at me.

"What. . .?" she whispered.

She was staring at me, but her eyes were blank, as if she wasn't actually seeing me.

"Ann, it's Joe," I said. "I'm here to look after you. Mam's here as well. You'll feel better soon, I promise."

I remembered what Mam had said about giving them water, so I lifted Ann's head up and held a cup to her lips.

"Take a sip," I said.

I gave her cheeks a gentle squeeze to open her mouth and let some of the water trickle in. She went slack, and some of the water dribbled out of the side of her mouth. She'd stopped coughing.

I put the cup down and put my ear to her mouth. The faint wheezing sound told me she was still breathing.

But then I noticed that her skin had the same purple tinge that I had seen on Arthur's gran's face, and I felt sick. What if we couldn't save her?

CHAPTER

Mam came and joined me at about half past seven. Dad dozed off now and then, but was more and more alert each time he woke up. His cough wasn't anywhere near as bad and his temperature was definitely down. I kept him supplied with water, while Mam concentrated on looking after my sister.

Ann hadn't opened her eyes again, and although she wasn't coughing as much, her breathing was very laboured. No matter how often Mam wiped her face, she stayed hot. Worst of all, her skin still had that awful purple tinge to it.

I was downstairs making a pot of tea when there was a knock at the front door. It was Doctor Campbell.

"How are they?" he asked, striding in.

He looked exhausted – his face was pale and he had dark shadows under his eyes.

"Dad's awake but Ann's still looking bad. Her skin's going purple."

I followed him up the stairs. He opened his bag and took out his stethoscope and a thermometer. He went to Ann first, listening to her lungs with his stethoscope and taking her temperature. Then he did the same with Dad. I felt Mam take hold of my hand and grip it tightly, anxious.

"Well, doctor?" she asked.

"Your husband seems to be over the worst, and with rest he should recover, but your daughter. . ." He shook his head. "With her medical history I worried this might be the case, so I managed to get her a bed at the infirmary. Sadly, one became available just an hour ago."

'Sadly' meant someone had just died. Was that what was going to happen to Ann? I looked at my sister, so small and frail, and I felt so helpless. Nothing in the war had prepared me for this. The flu wasn't an enemy you could shoot at.

"There are no ambulances free, so I'll take her in my car," continued Doctor Campbell.

"I'll come with you," said Mam. "I want to be with her."

"They won't let you into the ward," said Doctor Campbell.

"Then I'll sit in the waiting room," she replied.

The doctor put his hand on her shoulder.

"Mrs Henry, you'll be more use here looking after your husband. He still needs nursing."

I could see the struggle in Mam's eyes, torn between her husband and her little girl.

"I'll go," I said. "I'll stay in the waiting room. Then I can be there if . . . if there's any news."

Mam nodded.

"All right," she said, reluctantly.

Doctor Campbell packed his stethoscope and thermometer into his bag.

"Can you carry her, Joe?" asked Doctor Campbell. "My car's just outside."

We pulled up outside the entrance to the infirmary and Doctor Campbell lifted up Ann and carried her in, with me following. The entrance hall was full of people wearing masks and anxious expressions. I knew I must look the same. As Doctor Campbell carried Ann to the reception desk, the people waiting moved aside to let him through, nodding in silent greeting.

"I've brought Ann Henry in," Doctor Campbell announced. "I've arranged a bed for her."

The receptionist made a telephone call, and soon a nurse and a porter appeared pushing a trolley. They were both wearing masks of white gauze. The porter took Ann from Doctor Campbell and put her on the trolley, while the nurse handed a mask to the doctor.

"I'll see you in a moment, Joe," said Doctor Campbell, putting on the mask.

As I watched Ann's small, still body disappear into the lift and the doors clang shut, I felt a lump in my throat. Was this going to be the last time I saw my sister alive?

CHAPTER

I had been sitting in the infirmary's waiting room for almost three hours when Mam arrived. I was surrounded by anxious relatives like me, all hoping for good news. A few strings of tinsel and a small Christmas tree in the corner did little to cheer up the room. Because this flu was such a dangerous strain, the usual visiting hours had been cancelled. No one was allowed near the patients except the hospital staff. Maybe it was to stop people bringing flu germs into the hospital from outside. Maybe it was to stop visitors getting infected.

Mam put her hand on my arm.

"Any news?" she asked.

I shook my head.

"No news is good news," I said, trying to sound hopeful.

She didn't look convinced by that, but then I didn't feel convinced by it either.

"I'll take over," she said. "You go home and take care of your dad. Mrs Graham's checking on him at the minute."

"I'm happy to stay here," I said.

"Go home," she said. "Your dad wants to talk to you."

"What about?" I asked.

"Go home and you'll find out."

I looked at her, wondering how to explain my feelings. I didn't want to end up in another row with Dad, especially when he was so weak.

"Go home and talk to your dad," Mam repeated, firmer this time.

When I got home, Dad was sitting up in bed. He looked pale, but definitely seemed better.

"How's Ann?" he asked.

"They didn't tell me anything," I said. "Do you want me to make you a cup of tea?"

He jerked his thumb to the glass of water on the bedside table.

"This'll do me for the moment." He looked at me. "Are you just going to stand there?"

Here we go, I thought with a sinking heart. *He's going to have a go at me*. I was determined not to answer him back and get into a row. Not today, at least. I sat down.

"I was wrong," he said.

I felt bewildered. Had I heard him right?

"Wrong about what?" I asked.

"You," he said. "I was angry about you going off to war like that. Worrying your mother senseless."

"I went to help end the war. To get you home..." I started to protest.

He waved his hand to tell me to be quiet, and I shut up.

"I ain't got that much breath," he said. "I don't want to use it up arguing. What's done is done. What I wanted to say is, I was wrong about you. You always were a good boy, and now you're a good man."

He stopped, panting. When he'd got his breath back, he spoke again.

"I'm proud of you, Joe."

It was the last thing I'd expected to hear. In all my life, Dad had never admitted to being in the wrong.

I got up and went over to him, putting my hand gently on his shoulder. This didn't seem like the right time for shaking hands.

"I was wrong too," I admitted. "I shouldn't have gone off like I did. I didn't mean to hurt you and Mam."

He looked at me, then nodded. That speech, the longest I think I'd ever heard him say, had taken a lot out of him, but I saw the look in his eyes. For the first time since I'd got back, I saw love and affection there.

"I'd like to move back in," I said. "I'd like to come home."

He nodded again.

"I'm glad," he said and closed his eyes.

I sat beside him, reading the newspaper by his bed and fetching water when he asked for it. It felt good to be in the same room with my dad, peaceful and quiet for the first time in ages.

A couple of hours later, we heard the front door open and shut, and then footsteps coming up the stairs.

"That's your mam," said Dad. He tried to sit up, but he fell back on his pillows.

Mam came into the room, and I felt my stomach drop. Her face was wet with tears. I knew at once that it was all over. Ann was dead.

Then, through her tears, she smiled.

"She's all right," she burst out, starting to cry properly. "Her temperature is going down! Our girl's going to be all right!"

CHAPTER

Because people were still falling ill, the hospital needed every bed, so after two days we were asked to take Ann home to finish getting better. Next morning I went back to work and told George Potts about my sister.

"Finally some good news," said George. "Don't worry about hanging around this afternoon, Joe. Go and help your family bring your sister back from hospital."

"Thanks, George," I said. "I promise I'll be back at work tomorrow morning."

"Not here, you won't," said George, chuckling.

"Why?" I asked.

"Have you forgotten what day tomorrow is?"

I looked at him, puzzled, and then it suddenly hit me.

"Christmas Day!" I burst out.

George grinned. "How could you forget something like that?"

What with all the rows with my dad, and then Ann getting ill, I hadn't been thinking about Christmas at all. And somehow it had snuck up... Now it was tomorrow! I hadn't got any presents for Mam or Dad or Tim or Ann. I hadn't even got a card for them...

I'd arranged to meet Mam at the infirmary at one o'clock. She was already there, waiting for me when I arrived.

"They're getting Ann dressed now," she said. "Will you be able to carry her to the bus?"

"We're not getting the bus," I said. "We'll get a taxi."

Mam looked doubtful.

"Taxis cost money," she said.

"I have a job now," I told her. "We can afford it. We're getting a taxi."

When we got home I carried Ann up to her room and Mam made her comfortable in her bed. Dad and Tim followed us up the stairs, and we all made a fuss of her and tucked her in.

"Do you want anything, love?" Mam asked. "A drink? Some soup?"

"A story," said Ann, making us all laugh.

"Which one?" asked Mam.

"The one about the elves and the shoemaker."

Mam took Ann's book of fairy tales off the shelf and settled down to read. Dad, Tim and I went back downstairs, and Tim showed me the paper chains he'd been putting up around the house that afternoon under Dad's direction.

"For Christmas!" he said.

"I meant to get a tree," said Dad. "But then, the flu…"

"I'll get one," I said.

"There won't be many left," said Dad doubtfully.

"I'll find one," I promised.

I left Dad and Tim to carry on putting up decorations. We'd put up the same paper garlands, candles and cards on Christmas Eve every year since I could remember.

I put on my coat and scarf, and set off to find a tree. The paths were icy, and I had to be careful not to slip. There were no trees at the Jones's farm, where we normally bought them, but I found a man with a few small trees in the town square. I agreed a price and handed over the money, before slinging it over my shoulder, wincing as the needles prickled my cheek.

There were a couple of Christmas market stalls in the square too, and I used the last of my wages to pick up a few small presents for my family. It wasn't much, but it would be something for each of them to open tomorrow morning. Weighed down by the tree, with the presents tucked awkwardly in a paper bag under my arm, the walk home wasn't much fun. But when Tim opened the front door, the size of his grin let me know it had been worth the effort. My wages had gone, but at least the money had been spent on a good cause – bringing happiness to our home. After the long stretch of trouble we'd all had, we needed something to feel cheerful about.

*

"Happy Christmas!" we all chorused, clinking our glasses together.

Me, Mam, Dad, Tim, Arthur, Mrs Graham and even Ann were all sat round our dining-room table, paper crowns on our heads.

Everyone had liked the presents I'd bought – a comic annual for Tim, a bear glove puppet for Ann, some knitting patterns for Mam and a book about trains for Dad. Mam and Dad gave me a new jumper, along with a pair of thick leather gloves, which would be brilliant for when I was working on the roads.

We'd had a delicious roast dinner followed by a wonderful Christmas pudding, and were all feeling happy and full.

"Walter, could you say a few words?" asked Mam. "A special toast for Christmas."

We all turned to Dad, who sat looking uncertain for a moment.

"As you know, I don't really do speeches, so I'll keep it short. Let's raise a glass to the war being over. And coming home."

After we drank the toast, he turned to me and laid

a hand on my shoulder. "And now you, Joe. Let's have a toast from you."

I stared at him, taken aback that he'd handed the honour over to me. I lifted my glass in the air. "To no more wars," I said firmly.

Everyone raised their glasses too, and echoed my words.

"No more wars!"

HISTORICAL NOTE:

THE PEOPLE

Joe and his family are fictitious, but their experiences are based on historical accounts of people who experienced life in England, shortly after the World War One Armistice.

THE ARMISTICE

4th October 1918: The German government formally asked President Wilson of the USA for a ceasefire. Wilson put forward a fourteen-point peace programme, which the Germans were prepared to consider, but the British and French were unwilling to accept some of the proposals. When Wilson threatened to sign a separate peace treaty with Germany, the British and French agreed to talk terms.

4th November: The Battle of the Sambre (Belgium) was the last major attack of the Allied offensive on the Western Front. It involved the British First, Third and Fourth Divisions, and the French First Division. There were 10,000 German prisoners taken in one day. Along with the continuing US–French offensive at Meuse-Argonne in the south, this convinced the German Supreme Command that the war was lost, and they sought an armistice.

Despite this, some German units continued to mount a defence and the actual fighting continued in some areas.

5th November: Germany was informed of the Allies' Supreme War Council's agreement to an armistice based on the German acceptance of the terms of surrender.

7th November: The German delegation crossed the

front line in five cars and were then escorted for ten hours across northern France to a railway train, arriving at the train in the morning of 8th November. This train took them to a railway siding in the Forest of Compeigne. There they boarded a private railway carriage owned by the French military leader, Marshal Foch, to discuss terms for the Armistice.

9th November: Kaiser Wilhelm II abdicated the German throne and fled to Holland.

10th November: Armistice talks continued. The Germans were presented with the terms of surrender for them to sign. They were informed there would be no negotiations.

THOSE TAKING PART IN THE TALKS:

For the Allies:
Marshal Foch (French military commander); **General Weygand** (French military commander);

First Sea Lord Wemyss (British navy officer); **Deputy First Sea Lord Hope** (British navy officer); **Captain Marryat** (British navy officer).

For Germany:
Matthias Erzberger (politician); **Count Oberndorff** (foreign minister); **Major General Detlev von Winterfeldt** (army officer); **Captain Vanselow** (navy officer).

The document was signed at 5 a.m. on 11th November, to take effect at 11 a.m. on that day (the eleventh hour of the eleventh day of the eleventh month).

In many areas, the fighting continued up to the last moment. The last British fatality in action was a cavalryman from the Irish Lancers, shot by a sniper at Mons on 11th November.

In the immediate aftermath of the Armistice, peaceful evacuation of German-occupied territories on the Western Front was required within fourteen days. The Armistice initially ran for thirty-six days. It was formally renewed on a regular basis, with the proviso that German deviation from the terms could bring a resumption of hostilities at forty-eight hours notice.

This led to the Paris Peace Conference (18th January 1919), and finally to the Treaty of Versailles on 28th June 1919.

THE INFLUENZA EPIDEMIC OF 1918

The flu epidemic that started during the last year of the Great War, and continued afterwards, caused more deaths than the Great War itself.

The total number of deaths during the Great War (military and civilian, and those resulting from illnesses caused by the war) are estimated at 18 million.

It is estimated that the worldwide flu epidemic of 1918 and 1919 killed between 50 and 80 million people (four per cent of the world's population at that time).

It was called the Spanish flu, but it is now believed to have started in the Middle East battle zones during the spring of 1918, before spreading. In the days before antibiotics such as penicillin, flu could be fatal, especially for those with weakened respiratory systems. Sadly, many of the home cures people tried (such as vinegar) didn't work.

This flu was particularly strong, and twenty per cent of the people who caught it died. Up to that time with a flu epidemic, the death rate was only 0.1 per cent. Many young and otherwise healthy people died from the flu, because they hadn't had time to build up immunity to the virus, having not lived through previous flu epidemics.

ANTHEM FOR DOOMED YOUTH

by Wilfred Owen, 1917

What passing bells for these who die as cattle?
Only the monstrous anger of the guns
Only the stuttering rifles' rapid rattle
Can patter out their hasty orisons.
No mockeries now and for them, no prayers
  nor bells,
Nor any voice of mourning save the choirs –
The shrill, demented choirs of wailing shells
And bugles calling for them from sad shires.
What candles may be held to speed them all?
Not in the hands of boys but in their eyes
Shall shine the holy glimmer of goodbyes.
The pallor of girls' brows shall be their pall
Their flowers the tenderness of patient minds
And each slow dusk a drawing down of
  blinds.

Wilfred Owen was born in Shropshire in 1893. He taught in France from 1912, then joined the British Army in 1915. He was wounded on the Somme in 1916 and invalided back to Britain. He returned to France in 1918, and won the Military Cross for bravery. He was killed at the Battle of the Sambre just one week before the Armistice. He is considered one of the greatest war poets.

CATHERINE JOHNSON

1783

FREEDOM

**A GRIPPING FIRST-HAND ACCOUNT OF ONE OF
THE MOST DANGEROUS TIMES IN HISTORY**